JABARI JUMPS

To Larkin, who is already a great jumper,
and to her big brother, Rowan,
who uses his "bravery" every day

Copyright © 2017 by Gaia Cornwall. All rights reserved. No part of this book may be reproduced, transmitted, or stored in an information retrieval system in any form or by any means, graphic, electronic, or mechanical, including photocopying, taping, and recording, without prior written permission from the publisher. First edition 2017. Library of Congress Catalog Card Number pending. ISBN 978-0-7636-7838-8.

This book was typeset in Lora. The illustrations were done in pencil, watercolor, and collage, then colored digitally.

Candlewick Press, 99 Dover Street, Somerville, Massachusetts 02144. visit us at www.candlewick.com.

Printed in Humen, Dongguan, China. 17 18 19 20 21 22 APS 10 9 8 7 6 5 4 3 2 1

FSC
www.fsc.org
MIX
Paper from
responsible sources
FSC® C101537

JABARI JUMPS

Gaia Cornwall

CANDLEWICK PRESS

"I'm jumping off the diving board today," Jabari told his dad.
"Really?" said his dad.

The diving board was high and maybe a little scary, but Jabari had finished his swimming lessons and passed his swim test, and now he was ready to jump.

"I'm a great jumper," said Jabari, "so I'm not scared at all."

"It's okay to feel a little scared," said his dad. "Sometimes, if I feel a little scared, I take a deep breath and tell myself I am ready. And you know what? Sometimes it stops feeling scary and feels a little like a surprise."

Jabari loved surprises.

"Jabari! You did it!" said his dad.

"I did it!" said Jabari. "I'm a great jumper!
And you know what?"

"What?" said his dad.

"Surprise double backflip is next!"